And Then a Harvest Feast

And Then
a Harvest Feast

Story and pictures by
GEORGE DENNISON

A Sunburst Book
Farrar, Straus & Giroux

For Susie and Becky

Contents

And Then a Harvest Feast

Leaving/Arriving/Advice
from Moose

Dog met Cat in front of the supermarket. Cars were whizzing by and the air smelled bad.

"I can't stand this place any more," said Cat. "I'm off to the woods."

Just then Stork and Rabbit came out of the supermarket. Rabbit was chewing a carrot, but you couldn't hear the *munch munch* because he kept saying *phooey.*

"Look at the junk they call food," he said. He took another bite and said, "Phooey!"

"The city is so noisy I can't hear myself think," said Stork, "and that's a dreadful loss."

"Come along then," said Dog. "We're going back to the woods."

They heard a voice above their heads. "Me too!" it shouted. "I'll come with you!" It was Bird. He was flying in circles and coughing. "I haven't had a good meal in weeks," he shouted. "And the trees are getting sick."

"To the woods! To the woods!" cried Cat. But before they could move they heard a commotion behind them. Bear and Woodchuck and Mouse came running out of the supermarket shouting and waving their arms.

Bear was shouting, "To the woods! To the woods!"

Woodchuck was waving a leaf of spinach. "These greens aren't green," he shouted. "They're yellow!"

"They even charge you for the crumbs!" cried Mouse.

So Dog and Cat, and Rabbit and Stork, and Bird and Mouse, and Woodchuck and Bear went back to the woods together.

"But first," said Bear, "we ought to shake our fists at them and sing 'em a song they won't forget."

He made up a song, and they all stood together and shook their fists and sang:

14

Good-by to you,
   you terrible supermarket!
We're sick of your yellow greens,
we're sick of your stringy beans.
We hate your fake bread
and we hate your fake candy
and we hate your handy packages
that are not handy.
So good-by forever! Good-by!

"That's terrific," said Woodchuck. "Let's sing some more."

"Make up a verse," said Bear.

"Okay," said Woodchuck, and he sang:

Good-by to that music
   that comes out of the ceiling!

"Is that all?" said Bear.

"Isn't that enough?" said Woodchuck.

"A real song," said Stork, in his slow voice, "ought to have rhymes in it."

"Oh yeah?" said Woodchuck. And he sang:

Good-by to that music
   that comes out of the ceiling.
It sounds gooey.

"True," said Bear.

"That's not exactly a rhyme," said Stork.

"Try again," said Bear.

"Okay," said Woodchuck, and he sang very loudly:

Good-by to that music
    that comes out of the ceiling.
It sounds gooey.
Everything about you
    makes us say phooey.

"Bravo! Bravo!" said Bear. Woodchuck jumped up and down, and they sang it together, and Mouse yelled, "Yeah, go sit on your canned goods. Maybe they'll hatch!"

And they all marched off, laughing merrily, though no one had the slightest idea what they were going to do.

They walked a long time, and left the city far behind. Then they came to the woods and found a wide path and went in among the trees. It was quiet and shadowy. Everywhere they looked there were tree trunks, straight ones and leaning ones, big trees and little trees, and between the trees there were bushes of all kinds. Last year's leaves lay matted and moist on the ground.

They walked along happily, talking and whistling.

It was late spring. The forest was many shades of green.

"Ah!" said Dog. "How good the air is!"

Everyone breathed deeply and said, "Ah!"

There were lilies of the valley growing by the path, and jack-in-the-pulpits, and new ferns still coiled at the top like the heads of fiddles.

Stork stopped walking. He stood very tall and cocked his head.

"Are you listening to yourself think?" said Rabbit.

"No," said Stork. "I'm wondering what to do."

They stopped talking and stood there scratching their heads.

"What we need," said Bear, "is a good idea."

So they went to see their friend Moose, who lived alone by a pond in the woods. He was known to be wise and to have a great many good ideas.

"What's the difference between smart and wise?" said Woodchuck to Bear as they walked along.

"Oh, you have to be smart to be wise," said Bear, "but being smart is not enough, because most of the smart ones aren't wise."

"Why?" said Woodchuck.

"I don't know," said Bear.

The path grew narrow and somewhat darker in the shadows of the trees, and they had to go one at a time.

"We are on a deer trail," said Bear.

Woodchuck was still puzzled. "How do we know Moose is wise?" he said. "How do we know he's not just smart?"

"Moose is both smart *and* wise," said Bear. "We know he is smart because he has so many good ideas. And we know he is wise because he doesn't have to do anything about a single one of them, but is already perfectly contented."

When Bear answered Woodchuck like this, Woodchuck always said, "I see," whether he saw or not. And so he said, "I see."

Bird was flying high above the trees. He dived down and called to them, "We're almost there! I can see the pond!"

Soon all of them could see it. The sunlight twinkled through the trees and the water had the soft brown color of woodland ponds.

They were hot and thirsty and they jumped in the pond and swam about. Bear splashed up water and caught the sparkling drops in his mouth. Then they saw Moose, standing in a grassy field across the pond.

They called out to him, "Hello, Moose! Hello! We've come to see you!"

Moose raised his big head slowly and looked at them, calmly chewing a wad of grass.

They swam across to him, and he came down to the water and stood there chewing the grass. They climbed on some rocks and fallen trees.

"Moose," said Bear, "we have come to a

turning point in our lives. We want to talk to you and get some good ideas."

Moose looked at them one by one.

"Life in the city has made us unhappy," said Woodchuck.

"Yeah," said Mouse, "we're never going back to that terrible supermarket. They can sit on their canned goods for all we care."

"But what are we going to do?" said Dog. "How are we going to live?"

There was a long silence. Moose finished chewing and swallowed the grass. Everyone noticed how gigantic he was, and how his shaggy sides went in and out as he breathed. But his voice, when he finally spoke, wasn't frightening at all. It was actually very pleasant.

"Woodchuck," he said, "I have not seen you for a year. You are twice as big as you were."

"Yes," said Woodchuck, very pleased that Moose had noticed.

"And you, Bear," said Moose. "You have gained weight."

"Have I?" said Bear. He glanced curiously at his belly.

"But you, Bird," said Moose, "I don't know you at all. I have never seen you before."

"I am only one year old," said Bird.

Moose nodded. He lowered his head and took a drink of water from the pond. Then he raised his head and pointed to a nearby hill. "Beyond that hill," he said, "is another hill. And beyond that another. And beyond that another. And on that one there is an old farm, and nobody lives there. I suggest that you all move in and plant a garden. Share the work, share the food, and perhaps you will make sense of your lives."

He paused and said thoughtfully, "It will be very difficult to make sense of your lives. But do not be discouraged. Even a little sense is a remarkable thing." And he nodded slowly, agreeing with himself three whole times. Then he nodded once more. Then he put down his head and drank water again, and climbed out of the pond and went into the grassy field and lay down.

As they went away through the woods, Woodchuck said to Bear, "Why didn't Moose invite us to live at the pond with him?"

"Do you want to live at a pond?" said Bear.

"No," said Woodchuck, "but why didn't he invite us?"

"Moose likes to be alone," said Bear.

The House in the Woods

Even though Bird was only one year old, it was he who led them to the abandoned farm. When he flew up high, he could see everything for miles around. He kept diving down and calling, "This way! This way!"

And finally there it was, a big wooden house with a shingled roof and clapboard sides and two chimneys of faded red brick. There was moss on the roof. Years and years of sun and rain had turned the clapboards a handsome gray. A huge maple tree towered beside the house and the lacy shadows of its leaves lay across the roof. There were grassy fields all around the house, with apple trees and bushes, and there were low bushes growing under all the windows.

"Oh!" said Woodchuck. "It's beautiful!"

"My!" said Bear. "It's big enough for everyone!"

They ran right into it—Dog and Cat, and Woodchuck and Bear, and Rabbit and Bird and Stork and Mouse—and their voices could be heard everywhere, in the entryway and the cellar and all the downstairs rooms. "Look at this! A chair!" "Look at this! A bed!" "Look at this! A box!"

In the kitchen, which was very large, there was a big iron cookstove, a table and chairs, and a box for firewood, and shelves, and a sink with a pump, and an old kerosene lamp, and an iron frying pan hanging on a nail, and several pots, and a couple of buckets.

Woodchuck ran right through the kitchen and out the back door.

"Hey!" he called. "There's a well out here, and it's full of water!"

Bear went to look.

"I wonder who filled it up," said Woodchuck.

"Wells fill themselves up," said Bear. "The water comes from under the ground."

25

"My goodness!" said Woodchuck. He ran back into the house.

"Hey!" he called. "Here's a great big crock with a lid on it and I can't get it off!"

Bear went to look.

"What do you suppose is in it?" said Woodchuck.

"I would guess nothing at all," said Bear.

"If we're only guessing," said Woodchuck, "why guess that?"

"Very well," said Bear. "I guess it's full of blueberries."

"Oh boy!" said Woodchuck.

Bear lifted the lid.

"Phooey!" said Woodchuck. "Nothing at all."

"Exactly," said Bear. "But you wait and see. We will fill it with blueberries before the summer is over."

Just then they heard a voice they had never heard before. It said, "What are you doing in my house? Get out of my house!"

And Bear felt something hit him in the head. Woodchuck clapped his hand to his head, too, and said, "Ow!"

Soon everyone was holding his head. The floor was covered with nuts.

"Somebody's throwing nuts!" said Bear.

"There he is!" said Stork.

There was a hole in the ceiling, and sticking down through the hole was the head of a squirrel. His arm came down, too, and he threw another nut at Bear, but Bear just caught it in his mouth and ate it.

"What?" cried Squirrel. "First you break into my house, and now you eat my nuts! Clear out!"

"Is it really your house?" said Bear. "Do you use all of it?"

"Well, I don't use all of it," said Squirrel. "I have a secret little place up here in the attic."

"I've never been in an attic in all my life,"

said Rabbit. "I don't like high places."

"I like high places," said Squirrel. "I bet you don't like nuts, either."

"No, I don't," said Rabbit.

"What a dope!" said Squirrel. He threw a nut at Rabbit, but Bear leaned over and caught it in his mouth and ate it.

"Stop eating my nuts!" yelled Squirrel.

"Squirrel," said Stork, "we would like to live here. We would like to plant a garden, and share the work, and share the food, and make sense of our lives."

"Sense!" cried Squirrel. "Sense?" He laughed. "What's so good about sense?"

"You're a comedian," growled Cat. "What's wrong with sense?"

"Look here, Squirrel," said Bear. "Wouldn't you like to have someone to play with, and talk to, and sing songs with? You could work in the garden, too, and help eat the food."

Squirrel jumped out of the hole in the ceiling and landed on the stove, and jumped to the firewood box, and then to the back of a chair, and then to the window ledge, laughing all the while.

"Play with?" he said. "Is anybody here fast enough to play with me? You're a bunch of slowpokes, but I'm quick as a wink."

"Well, I'm quick as half a wink," said Cat, "which makes me twice as quick as you!" And he leaped at Squirrel and almost caught him, and chased him around and around the kitchen. When Dog saw Cat running like that he began to shake all over, then he growled very loud and chased after Cat. Rabbit hid in the corner, and Mouse hid by the table leg. Bird perched on the highest shelf. Finally Bear said, "What a racket! Stop now! Stop, I say!"

When Bear spoke in his deep voice everyone listened. Cat stopped chasing Squirrel and Dog stopped chasing Cat, and they stood there puffing, waiting to see what Bear would say.

Bear said only, "We must live in peace. Let us sit down and figure out what we are going to do."

"Okay," said Squirrel, "but one thing— nobody eats my food."

"Who wants your old nuts?" said Dog. "Bah!"

And everyone said, "Okay, we won't eat your food."

"Promise?" said Squirrel.

"Promise," they said.

And so they sat down in the kitchen and talked a long while, and decided that Stork would fly away immediately to visit a farm.

He'd spend the next day with the farmers and learn how to plant seeds and make things grow. And he'd bring back as many seeds as he could carry.

"Which will be quite a few seeds," said Stork, "as my wings are very powerful. And when I get back . . ."

"When he gets back," Bear whispered to Woodchuck, "he will make a speech about gardening. Stork loves to make speeches."

"And when I get back," said Stork, "I will make a speech about gardening."

After Stork had flown away, the others looked at the apple trees, and the maple trees, and the birch trees; they walked in the grassy fields and looked at the stone walls that bordered them. And wherever they went, they looked back at the house, and it looked just fine from every angle. The sun was going down and all the trees and bushes cast long skinny shadows.

They built a fire in the cookstove that night, not to keep warm, for it wasn't cold, but just to see how it worked. And when darkness came and all the windows were black, they lit the kerosene lamp. Bear told a ghost

30

story that made them all shiver. And Wood-chuck said, "Hey, Squirrel, do you think there are any ghosts in this house?"

Squirrel said, "Yes, there probably are. There used to be a famous one. Years ago a strange old squirrel lived here all alone. And when he died, he came back and haunted the place. You could hear him chewing nuts up in the attic, but when you went to look, you couldn't see anything."

31

Nobody shivered.

Squirrel got angry and told the story all over again in a much louder voice.

". . . and when you went to look," he shouted, "you couldn't see anything!"

There was just silence. But at last Mouse said, in a small voice, "Is he still here?"

Squirrel didn't answer him. But he whispered in Mouse's ear, "You can come up to the attic with me and I'll show you my secret food supply." Out loud he said, "Nobody else can come!" And they went off.

Now everybody was getting sleepy. Bear was happy, and he began to sing quietly in his deep, mellow voice:

Our house is on a hillside,
moss is growing on the roof.
A great big maple gives us shade,
the water in the well is sweet.

"Gee, Bear," said Woodchuck, just before he fell asleep, "there weren't any rhymes at all in that song."

"No," said Bear. "Songs don't have to rhyme."

Little Specks of Stuff

Not everybody knew what a shovel was, or what a rake looked like, or a hoe. But Bear and Dog knew, and so whenever somebody found something he put it in a pile beside the house, and then Bear and Dog picked out the useful tools. They spent the day looking for things.

Stork came back before supper. There were lovely white clouds in the sky, and the sun was still bright. Stork came planing in over the treetops. He glided to a maple stump near the house, and then flapped his wings gustily and hovered right over it, and his long legs dangled down, and he settled on the stump as lightly as a feather, and shivered his wings and folded them behind him, looking very pleased with himself, for they had all gathered round him shouting, "Here's Stork! Good old Stork!"

"My friends," he said, "I brought plenty of seeds."

They shouted, "Hurrah for Stork!"

"Thank you," said Stork. "And I talked with the farmers, as a result of which I have a complete theoretical knowledge of gardening."

"What does theoretical mean?" whispered Woodchuck to Bear.

"It means you know all about it, probably, even though you never did it," whispered Bear.

"The first thing," Stork went on, "is to figure out where to put the garden. Now . . . it should not face the north, and it should not face the east, and it should not face the west. It should face the south. That way it will get the most sunlight, and sunlight is vitally important. Without sunlight nothing would grow—no grass, no trees, no flowers, no vegetables. The garden should slope gently to the south . . ."

"What does slope mean?" whispered Woodchuck to Bear.

"It means if you drop a ball at one end of

the garden it will roll downhill to the other end," whispered Bear.

"The slope of the garden will give good drainage," said Stork, "by which I mean that rain water will not make puddles. Puddles are bad for gardens."

"Phooey!" said Squirrel. "You can do all kinds of things with puddles."

"But not in gardens," said Stork. "They will make the vegetables rot. And we do not want them to rot, we want to eat them."

"True," said Dog.

"And we must dig up the ground with shovels, and break up the clumps with hoes, and we must take out the grass roots and stones with our rakes. Then when the soil is crumbly

35

and small we put in the seeds, and we must put them in rows so we can walk between them to take out the weeds, and later on to pick the vegetables. And when we plant the seeds we mustn't put them too deep, or they'll rot, and mustn't put them too shallow, or the rain will wash them out. A good rule is, you put them about as deep as four times the size of the seed."

"What a bunch of dopes!" said Squirrel. "All that work when you could eat nuts and get them free for the picking. They grow in the woods."

"Be quiet," said Cat, "or I'll put a kink in your tail."

"Hush," said Bear.

"Right after we plant the seeds," said Stork, "we should put water on the garden."

"Now they're lugging water," muttered Squirrel. Cat looked at him, and Bear patted Cat on the head.

"And I have bad news for you, Bird," Stork went on. "You mustn't eat worms in the garden, or even near the garden, because worms are — "

"Oh, no!" said Bird. "You mean I can't eat worms!"

"You can't eat worms," said Stork, "because worms are — "

"Worms are delicious!" said Bird.

"That wasn't what I was going to say," said Stork. "Worms are the gardener's best friend."

"I am the worms' best friend," said Bird. "I love them."

"You mean you love to eat them," said Dog. "If we all had friends like that, we wouldn't be here."

"You see, Bird," said Stork, "worms crawl around in the ground and keep it nice and crumbly, and they're always eating it just as if it were food, and when it passes out of them it's just perfect for the garden. So you mustn't eat worms."

"All right," said Bird.

"Eat bugs," said Stork.

"Yes," said Bird.

"Eat caterpillars," said Stork.

"Yes," said Bird.

"But don't eat worms."

"I'll do my best," said Bird.

"Now," said Stork, "I will lay out some seeds on this stump so you can look at them. They are quite amazing."

They all crowded around and looked at the seeds. And indeed they were amazing. Some were so tiny they looked like almost nothing.

"But what is this stuff?" said Woodchuck.

"These are the seeds," said Stork.

"But they're just little specks of stuff," said Woodchuck. "I could eat them all in one mouthful."

"But I just told you," said Stork, "we must plant them, and water them, and they will grow by themselves." He pointed to the different seeds. "These become carrots. These become lettuce. These are beans. Here's peas, corn, squash, onions."

"I don't believe it," said Woodchuck. "All those big things come out of these little tiny things?"

"It's true," said Bear. "Even the biggest trees come from tiny seeds. And the grass comes from seeds. And the flowers."

"Really?" said Woodchuck.

"Yes, really," said Stork.

"Well, where do the seeds come from?" said Woodchuck.

"Everything makes its own seed," said Bear. "The grass makes grass seed, the trees make tree seed . . . that's the way it goes."

"But how did it all get started?" said Woodchuck.

"Ah," said Bear. "Nobody knows."

"Now, my friends," said Stork, "let us begin."

They took their shovels and hoes and rakes and began breaking the sod downhill from the house, where the land sloped gently to the south. They grunted and sang and sweated . . .

all but Squirrel. Squirrel frolicked in the trees and stretched out on a limb and watched them and ate a nut. He sang a song to them, too.

> *Nuts are free,*
> *nuts are yummy.*
> *Somebody here*
> *is an awful dummy.*

And Cat threw down his shovel and chased Squirrel, and Dog threw down his hoe and chased Cat. But nobody caught anybody.

Bird on Trial

It took them several days to break up the sod and rake out the stones and grass roots. Bird tried very hard not to eat worms, but often when somebody would turn over a clump of dirt, a juicy fat worm would be lying there, and Bird would pounce on it and gobble it up. He just couldn't resist, especially if the worm wiggled, and of course most of them did wiggle. Then he would say, "I'm sorry." And he really was sorry, but he kept doing it so much that finally the others got mad at him.

"We must take drastic measures," Stork said. "Bird keeps breaking one of our most important rules. He must be punished, or he will never learn to stop breaking it. Perhaps we will be forced to build a jail and put him in it. He should certainly stand trial, and if he is found guilty we must punish him."

"What does guilty mean?" said Woodchuck.

"It means he really did it," said Stork.

"But we know he did it," said Woodchuck.

"It's not official," said Stork. "If we're going to punish him, it has to be official. He has to stand trial. He has to go before a judge and jury."

Woodchuck didn't understand any of that, and neither did Mouse or Rabbit. So Stork explained it.

"First," he said, "we have rules. We have to have rules, otherwise everything would be a mess. And the rules are for all of us, not just some of us. Everybody has to follow the rules . . ."

"Wait a minute," said Dog. "I don't follow this worm rule."

"You mean you've been eating worms?" said Stork.

"No," said Dog. "I didn't say I was *breaking* the rule. I just said I wasn't following it. Worms!

Ugh! I can't stand them. That rule doesn't have anything to do with me."

"Good point," said Bear.

"On the contrary," said Stork. "We are talking about breaking the rules. Bird broke a rule. He has to stand trial. A trial is when you have a judge and a jury. You have to have two lawyers, too. One of them says Bird really did it and ought to be punished. The other one says Bird didn't do it and should not be punished. Then the jury thinks it over. They have to argue about it and decide if he really did it. If they say he's guilty, then that's that—he's guilty. Then the judge says what the punishment will be. If you want to have a really bad punishment, you build a jail and put the guilty one in it and lock the door so he can't get out. And then after a while you let him out."

"That sounds awful," said Woodchuck.

"Exactly," said Stork. "That's what keeps the guilty one from breaking the rules again. Life is not easy. Bird must stand trial. I will be the judge."

Bird said, "I'm scared."

Bear said, "Don't worry. I will be your lawyer."

"But I really did it, you know," said Bird. "I'm guilty."

They went into the house, and Stork took the long-handled broom and held it upside down. He jumped on the big iron stove and said, "This is where the judge sits. The jury sits over there. Bird and his lawyer sit down there. Cat, you be the other lawyer. You sit there."

And so Rabbit and Mouse and Woodchuck and Dog were the jury. Stork pounded the broom handle on the stove and said, "Court is now in session."

"What's a court?" said Woodchuck.

"We are the court," said Stork. "Bird, you will be called the defendant, because you have to defend yourself. Come up and sit in this chair by the stove. That chair will be called the stand."

"Bird will be called defendant, chair will be called stand!" yelled Woodchuck. "Why don't we call Bird Bird and call the chair a chair!"

Stork pounded on the stove. "No talking in court," he said. "Come, Bird."

So Bird went up and sat in the chair. And Stork said, "What is your name?"

"But you know my name," said Bird.

"Please answer the question," said Stork. "You are in court now."

"My name?" said Bird.

"Yes," said Stork, "your name."

"My name is Bird!" yelled Bird.

"Excellent," said Stork. "Now . . . where do you live?"

"But you know where I live!" yelled Bird. "I live right here in this house!"

"Excellent," said Stork. "Now then, Bird, you are accused of eating worms in the garden. Are you guilty or not guilty?"

"I ate them all right," said Bird. "I'm sorry."

Bear jumped up and said, "There! You see! He did it and he's sorry. Now let's get back to work."

"Court will come to order," said Stork. "Lawyer Cat will say a few words."

Cat jumped up and put his hands on his hips and walked back and forth. "This Bird is guilty all right," he said. "He admits he's guilty, and he looks like he's guilty, and I bet if we cut open his belly we'd find a hundred and fifty worms in it."

Bird grabbed his belly and said, "Ow!"

"Don't talk like that, Cat," said Bear.

"This Bird," said Cat, "is what we call a repeater."

"Another new name," said Woodchuck.

"I mean," said Cat, "that he not only committed a crime, he did it again and again and again."

"I'll try harder," said Bird.

Bear jumped up and said, "Good idea! Now let's get back to work!"

"Yeah," said Mouse. "I'm tired of sitting in one place."

"I wish the carrots were up," said Rabbit.

"They aren't even planted yet," said Dog.

Stork pounded the stove with his broom. "Order in the court!" he said. "Have you finished, Lawyer Cat?"

"No," said Cat. "This Bird should be found guilty by the jury, and he should be put in jail, or we won't have a single worm left in that garden. That is all."

"Good speech," said Stork.

"Bad speech," said Bird.

"Now Lawyer Bear will say a few words," said Stork.

Bear stood up. "Members of the jury," he said, "I will show you that there is no great problem here. Please look at my hand. What am I holding?"

Dog and Woodchuck and Mouse and Rabbit looked at his hand.

"You're holding a worm," said Rabbit.

"Correct," said Bear. "Now I will hold this worm in front of Bird, and if he does not eat it, it will prove that he can control himself at least some of the time, and in my opinion that is good enough. After all, Bird likes to eat bugs, too, and there are thousands of bugs, and lots of them are bad for the garden. Now then, Bird . . . look right at this worm and let us see what you'll do."

Bear held the worm in front of Bird, and Bird looked at it and gulped, and shivered, and closed his beak tightly and looked at Bear.

"Bravo!" said Bear.

"Hurrah for Bird!" cried the jury.

"Order in the court!" shouted Stork. "Now we will hear from the jury."

But before the jury could say anything, a beautiful song came through the open window. It was coming from the trees not far away. Another bird was singing there. Bird cocked his head and listened. Then he lifted his beak and opened his throat and began to sing too, loud and long, and the jury clapped their hands and cried, "What a beautiful song!" "Bird's a champion singer!" Even Cat opened his mouth in amazement. "Terrific song," he said. Everyone shouted, "Bravo, Bird! Bravo!" and Bird flew away through the open window, and all the others went out of the house, shaking their heads and talking delightedly.

"What *brio*!"

"What cadenzas!"

A Lesson of Silence

The soil in the garden was soft and crumbly now, and it was time to plant the seeds. Stork made long straight furrows with his beak, and the others came behind him, dropping in seeds, covering them with soil, and patting the soil to make it firm so the first roots would be sure to catch hold. And then Bear and Dog came along with buckets and splashed water carefully over the buried seeds.

Bear and Stork went into the house to get supper ready, but the others sat down beside the garden. They were still there an hour later.

"Good heavens!" said Bear. He leaned out

49

the window and called to them, "What are you doing?"

"Nothing's happening," answered Wood-chuck.

"Not a single carrot," shouted Rabbit.

Bear laughed and said, "Of course not. It takes a little while."

"How long is that?" said Woodchuck.

"Well . . . I don't know exactly," said Bear. He turned to Stork. "How long does it take?" he asked.

"Well," said Stork, "the farmers said 'by and by.'" He leaned out the window and yelled, "Things will be up by and by."

"How long is that?" said Dog.

"It's a whole lot longer than a little while," shouted Stork, and he pulled his head in the window.

And so they decided not to watch the garden. But they went out and looked at it next day, and still nothing had happened. And they went the day after that, and there was nothing. And they went the next day, and still nothing.

"I told you those seeds were too small," said Woodchuck.

"Listen, Stork," said Cat, "are you sure you didn't get mixed up when the farmers talked to you?"

"I never get mixed up," said Stork. But he didn't look very happy.

They sat around in the kitchen that night and just moped. Squirrel offered them nuts to cheer them up, but nobody wanted any.

"Out of respect for your misery," said Squirrel, "I will go up to the attic and be happy where you can't see me."

"Maybe we put too much water on," said Dog.

"Maybe we didn't put on enough," said Bear.

"At least Bird got a few worms out of it," said Cat.

"I'm sorry," said Bird.

And they just sat there moping.

The next day they went into the garden, and there was nothing. And the day after that, and the day after that day—nothing, nothing at all.

"Maybe those weren't seeds at all," cried Woodchuck. "Maybe they were just little specks of stuff. I should have eaten them!"

They lay on the grass and looked at the sky, and didn't say anything. Stork felt especially bad. Maybe he *had* gotten mixed up.

Suddenly Bear sat up and said, "This is stupid! We shouldn't just lie here. Let's go and talk with Moose."

Woodchuck sat up, too. "Yeah!" he said. "Let's go see Moose."

They all jumped up, and went as fast as they could down the forest path.

When they got to the pond they couldn't see Moose. They shouted and called his name, and jumped in the water and swam across and climbed on the rocks and fallen trees. And then they saw him. He was resting in the shadows of the trees. He stood up slowly, and calmly came to the water's edge. He was so big and powerful that he pushed right through the bushes and small trees.

They all began talking at once, and Moose

just stood there and looked at them.

"We dug up our garden," said Bear, "and Stork brought seeds from the farmers, and we planted them and watered them . . ."

"I listened carefully to the farmers' instructions," said Stork.

"We did everything just right," said Woodchuck.

"But now a long time has gone by," said Dog, "and nothing has happened."

"Not one single carrot," said Rabbit.

They talked until they had talked themselves out, and then they waited to see what Moose would say. But he just stood there and looked at them, breathing deeply and calmly, and they watched his shaggy sides go in and out.

"What should we do?" said Stork.

Moose said nothing.

"Can't you help us?" said Rabbit.

Moose looked at him, and then looked at all of them. They stood like that for several minutes. Finally Moose lowered his head and took a long drink of water. He raised his head and swallowed it. He looked at them again. Then he turned around and walked slowly into the woods and lay down in the shadows of the trees.

Cat's mouth dropped open in amazement. So did Dog's. Mouse and Woodchuck looked at each other. Stork and Bird groaned. Rabbit just sat there. But Bear smiled foolishly and hung his head.

They swam across the pond without talking, and went silently up the forest path hanging their heads.

As they got near home, Cat yelled, "That ding-danged Moose! Who does he think he is?"

"What kind of a friend is he?" shouted Mouse. "We need help and he won't help us!"

"Moose never said he was our friend," said Bear.

"Well, what is he then?" said Dog.

"Moose is Moose," said Bear.

They went into the house and started banging the chairs around, and banging the pots and pans, getting ready for supper. Stork made a pot of soup, but he stirred it so angrily that a lot splashed out.

They sat down to eat, and they kept talking angrily about Moose—everyone but Bear.

Finally Stork said, "But what did he *mean*?"

"What do you mean what did he mean?" said Woodchuck. "He didn't say *anything*!"

"That's just it," said Stork. "What did he mean by that?"

They all stopped talking.

Cat said, "Yes. What did he mean?"

Woodchuck said, "Bear, why are you smiling?"

Bear said, "Because I think he did mean something."

Dog said, "Yes, he surely did."

And they all stopped talking and sat there thinking.

It rained that night, and the house creaked and tinkled. The rain pattered on the roof and hit scratchily against the windows. It was still raining the next morning. And then the rain stopped. The air was delicious. It was full of the odors of the woods, yet it was clear and bright. And then the sun came out. And there was sun the next day too.

Everyone got up as soon as it was light. Bear got up last, because he liked to lie there and stretch and make noises and think about his dreams. He was doing all this when he heard a lot of voices, a lot of shouting and laughing, and voices saying, "Hurrah! Hurrah!" He could hear Woodchuck shouting, "Green things! Green things!" and Stork saying, "Don't eat them, Woodchuck! Not yet, Woodchuck!"

Bear rushed out. The sky was bright blue

and his friends were gathered by the garden in the morning sunlight. They were jumping and waving their arms. Bird was flying around and around, chirping and twittering.

"Look at the garden!" yelled Woodchuck to Bear.

Tiny green plants sparkled in all the rows.

"I told you those seeds were amazing!" shouted Stork.

"Hurrah for Stork!" shouted Dog.

"Hurrah for Stork!" they shouted. "Hurrah for green things! The garden is up!"

"Moose was right!" shouted Woodchuck. "What a wise old Moose!"

"Hurrah for seeds!" shouted Dog.

"I told you they were amazing!" shouted Stork.

"They're amazing, all right," shouted Woodchuck. "Hurrah for those amazing little specks of stuff! I could have eaten them all in one mouthful!"

"You'll have millions of mouthfuls!" shouted Bear.

"Millions of mouthfuls!" everybody shouted.

And then they heard a voice in the trees. Squirrel was skipping along the branches making faces at them and singing a song.

> *Gardeners are dopey,*
> *gardeners are mad,*
> *but dopey gardeners happy*
> *beat dopey gardeners sad.*

He laughed and threw a shower of nuts at them. They laughed too, and dodged the nuts, and shouted, "Hurrah for Squirrel!"

Politics/Songs

Everyone remembered how Stork had flown away to the farmers and had listened to their instructions and had brought back the seeds. And now that the garden really was growing, they paid Stork many compliments. Dog would say, "Good job, Stork." And Stork would say, "Yes, indeed. Thank you, thank you."

And Cat would say, "Couldn't get along without you, old boy."

And Stork would say, "Yes, indeed. Thank you, thank you."

Stork enjoyed it so very much that he began to walk around rather proudly, with his wings folded behind his back. Sometimes he'd pick a place he knew they'd all pass by, and he'd just stand there and wait for their compliments, saying, "Thank you. Yes, indeed. Thank you." And if they forgot to compliment him, he would find little ways of reminding them. He would talk about seeds, or about gardening, but instead of calling it gardening he would call it "agriculture."

He looked more dignified than ever. He learned to smile in a very dignified way, and his voice became deeper and extremely dignified. And then he announced that the time had come to elect a president, and he said that he himself would make an excellent president.

"Sure, Stork," said Woodchuck. "What's a president?"

They had just finished supper. They were lying on the grass in front of the house. Stork was the only one standing.

"I will explain it to you," he said in his new, very dignified voice, and they all knew that Stork was going to make a speech.

Before, when Stork made speeches, he started right in and just made the speech. But now he cleared his throat three times, clasped his wings behind his back, and stood very tall.

He began by saying, "My friends, fellow citizens."

"My friends, fellow citizens," he said, "the question has been asked, what is a president? A president is . . . a president is . . . well, I would say that a president is the one who cares most what is happening. Yes, indeed. He cares very much about what is happening to everyone."

"Very good," said Bear. "It's nice to be cared about."

"Gee, Stork," said Woodchuck, "do you mean you really care what happens to me?"

"Yes, of course," said Stork, "I am deeply concerned."

"And if I got hurt, you'd come and help me?" said Woodchuck.

"Yes, exactly," said Stork.

"Gee," said Woodchuck, "that's really nice."

"But, Stork," said Bear, "you'd help him anyway, wouldn't you? You don't have to be president to do that."

"That's true," said Stork. "Yes, indeed. But you must remember, Woodchuck is just one person. A president cares about everybody."

"But, Stork," said Dog, "we all care about everybody."

"Ah," said Stork, "you care, yes, but what can you *do* about it? A president is able to *do* something. A president thinks up good ideas."

"So do I," said Cat.

"Me too," said Mouse.

"A president makes laws," said Stork.

"Uh-oh," said Bird. "I haven't eaten hardly any worms at all, Stork."

"No, he hasn't," said Bear.

"By laws," said Stork, "I only mean *rules*. And I don't mean that a president actually makes them. He just thinks them up and then everybody talks about them and decides what they want to do."

"But, Stork," said Cat, "you can already do that. We can all do that."

"Well," said Stork, "I will give you another example. For example, things we all care about. For example, the condition of the house we all live in. For example, I noticed this morning that a window was broken."

"Did you fix it?" asked Bear.

"No," said Stork. "I thought I would tell you about it and we could discuss the matter."

"Talk won't keep the rain out," said Cat. "You should have fixed it, Stork."

"Do you expect me to fix it right in the middle of a speech!" said Stork.

"If you were president," said Mouse, "would you fix it?"

"Of course," said Stork. "Rather . . . I'd *find* somebody to fix it. That's another thing that presidents do. They find people to do things."

"How would you do that?" said Cat. "Do you know who the best window fixer is?"

"No," said Stork.

"Well, how would you find out?" asked Dog.

"I'd ask different people," said Stork. "For example, I'd ask Cat, since he knows a lot."

"So go ahead and ask me," said Cat.

"Very well, Cat," said Stork, "who *is* the best window fixer?"

"I won't tell you," said Cat.

"What!" said Stork. "Why won't you tell me?"

"Why should I?" said Cat. "You aren't going to fix it."

"But I'd tell the window fixer it's broken," said Stork.

"He already knows," said Cat.

"But how do we know he'll fix it?" said Stork.

"Ask him," said Cat.

"But I don't know who he is!" said Stork.

"Then you can't help us," said Cat. And he turned to Dog and said, "Will you fix it, old sport?"

Dog smiled and said, "Sure."

"Gee whiz, Stork," said Woodchuck, "what *does* a president do?"

"Another example!" shouted Stork. "That big rock in the orchard. It should be moved! If I were president I would find somebody to figure out how to move it, and then I would tell somebody to move it, and then—"

Bear interrupted him. "Stork," he said, "there isn't any rock in the orchard."

"You are mistaken," cried Stork.

"Cat figured out how to move it," said Bear. "And just before supper, Dog and I moved it."

"I am very pleased to hear it," said Stork.

"We are *all* pleased to hear it!" shouted Mouse.

"Especially me," said Bird, "because there were bugs under it and I ate them."

"Why the ding-dang dickens do you *want* to be president?" said Cat.

"Why?" shouted Stork. "Why?" He had forgotten all about being dignified. He was shouting and waving his wings.

"Why?" he shouted. "Because then you get to make speeches, that's why! And everybody listens. And even if they don't believe you, they aren't supposed to say anything. And you get a special big house to live in, and people do everything for you, they fix your food, and brush your feathers, and everywhere you go people say, 'Hurrah, here comes the president!'"

"Wow!" said Woodchuck. "That sounds pretty good!"

"You bet it's good!" shouted Stork.

"Can anybody be president?" asked Rabbit.

"Anybody can try," said Stork, "but you have to win votes. The one who gets the most votes gets to be president."

"What's a vote?" said Woodchuck.

"A vote is just your chance to say who you want to be president."

"Me!" shouted Woodchuck.

"Me!" shouted Rabbit.

Everybody shouted "Me!" and Bear sat there laughing. "Everybody wants to be president," he said.

"It's nonsense," said Stork. "They don't understand the duties. They have no conception of the work."

"But, Stork," said Cat, "you haven't told us a single ding-danged thing the president actually *does*."

"He gets jobs for his friends!" shouted Stork.

"We already have jobs," said Bear. "We work in the garden."

"He talks with other presidents," said Stork. "That's what he does, and nobody else can do it, only the president."

"What do they talk about?" asked Cat.

"Presidential business!" said Stork. "And you aren't allowed to know!"

"But then, Stork," said Bear, "if your business is with other presidents, what are you doing here with us?"

"Yeah," said Mouse. "Go talk to them! Get *their* votes!"

"Alas," said Stork. "They all vote for themselves, just like you."

"Hey, look!" said Cat. "The sun is going down. We don't have much time."

"Good heavens," said Bear, jumping up. "Let's get busy!"

They all jumped up and ran off to the garden. There was something special they wanted to do. The plants were growing well now; they were getting bigger and greener. It was time to pull some so that the others would have room to grow. And the special thing was that you could eat the ones you pulled.

Stork was standing there all alone. He heard a noise in the trees and looked up. Squirrel was sitting on a limb.

"Alas," said Stork. "Nobody wants a president."

Squirrel was shaking his head.

"You're going to throw a nut at me, aren't you?" said Stork.

"Yep," said Squirrel. And he did, and hit poor Stork in the head.

Woodchuck came running back from the garden. "Stork! Stork!" he called. "Come and help us. We could use that nice long beak of yours. These little green things are delicious. Wow!"

"Here I come, here I come," said Stork, and he galloped after him, flapping his big wings and stretching his long bony legs.

Now everywhere in the garden you could hear a pleasant crunching and munching and sighing. Woodchuck kept saying, "Wow! Oh boy!"

There were tender young leaves of lettuce, and shoots of bean plants, and tiny onions, and small leaves of chard.

"And to think it's all extra," cried Bear. "My friends, I toast you with this onion." He held it up, then popped it in his mouth. And everywhere you could hear, "I toast you with

this radish!" "I toast you with these bean
stalks!" "I toast you with this lettuce!"

The sun went down and the moon came up,
and the moon was so bright they kept right on
plucking green things and popping them into
their mouths. They were saying, "Mmmmm,"
and they were chewing and swallowing and
saying, "Ah," and it sounded almost like music.
Then they lay on the grass in front of the house
and looked at the moon and stars. Somebody

started singing and they all joined in. They sang *Sweet Barbara Allen*, and *Skip to My Lou*, and *She'll Be Comin' Round the Mountain*. They sang all the songs they could think of. They even sang Christmas carols, though Christmas was a long way off.

"You know what we ought to do?" said Stork. "When harvest time comes, we ought to have a harvest feast and invite everybody from miles around."

"That's a really good idea, Stork," said Bear.

They sang *God Rest Ye Merry, Gentlemen* and *Deck the Halls with Boughs of Holly*.

"A harvest feast," said Dog.

They had already sung *Good King Wenceslas*, but they sang it again.

Crickets were chirping and frogs were making a thrumming music somewhere nearby.

They sang another song.

You could see the hills in the distance, dark at the bottom, but so light at the top that a few large pines stood out against the clouds.

The moon was high. The smaller stars were invisible, but in the far corners of the sky the planets and the larger stars glowed like lamps.

Deep Summer

So many things were blooming and growing! There were great green leaves of rhubarb beside the house. The raspberry bushes had blossomed, and now there were blossoms on the blackberries. There were wild things to eat, tangy, delicious strawberries, and the young green leaves of pigweed and sorrel.

"You see," said Squirrel. "The whole place is a garden. All you have to do is pick what you want and turn somersaults." He was frolicking all the time.

There were weeds to pull in the garden, and water had to be carried when there wasn't any rain, but that didn't take long, and the days were filled with pleasure. They wandered through the fields and woods and ate wild things and waded in the streams. They swam in all the nearby ponds and played games that sometimes took all day to finish.

After the blossoms fell, the berries began to form, and soon they were ripe—first the plump red raspberries, then the shiny, bumpy blackberries, and then the sparkling round elderberries that grew in clusters so heavy the slender limbs bent down like arches.

The farmers had told Stork how to gather berries and cook them in a pot and make jam.

"There is nothing so good on a cold winter morning," he said, "as a cup of cocoa and a piece of toast with jam."

They gathered eight buckets of raspberries, and made a fire in the stove, and got out their biggest pots and boiled the berries, and they put the jam in jars and put the jars on the shelves, and licked the spoons and pots, and then washed them in the stream, and took baths in the stream, and felt wonderfully good.

These were the deep, still days of summer, yellow and blue and green. There were bird songs, the buzz of insects and bees, the rustling of the wind in the trees, but often it all blended together and seemed almost like silence, or the beating of a heart.

One day Bear was lying in the grass near the garden talking with Woodchuck. They were watching the bees go from plant to plant and flower to flower.

"They are gathering a sweet juice called nectar," said Bear, "and they will take it away to where they live—probably in a hollow tree—and there they will make honey, which is simply delicious. In fact, it is extremely delicious stuff. You see how they fly away always in the same direction?

"Good heavens!" said Bear, and he jumped up and ran after the bees. He ran so fast that Woodchuck could not keep up. He simply vanished into the woods. A few minutes later he came out of the woods, running full tilt.

"Buckets!" he yelled. "Get buckets!"

And he rushed past Woodchuck into the house, and came out with buckets in both hands, and rushed past Woodchuck again, and vanished into the woods.

"What a speed demon!" said Woodchuck.

"What does he want?" said Rabbit.

"Buckets," said Woodchuck.

Bird was standing there too, and soon all the others came over.

"I mean," said Rabbit, "what does he want the buckets for?"

"Bees," said Woodchuck.

But that didn't make sense, so they all ran into the woods to see what Bear was doing.

They found him standing beside a stumpy hollow tree. He had pulled down part of the tree and it lay on the ground. There was a loud, furious buzzing in the air, and swarms of black dots whirled this way and that. Bear was reaching into the stump and pulling out something with his paw. He kept the bucket ready, but instead of putting the stuff into the bucket, he kept putting it into his mouth. The whirling black dots were bees. There were thousands and thousands of them. They dashed angrily at Bear and crawled over him in great swarms.

"Don't go any closer," said Stork. "A bee sting hurts something awful."

Even the buzzing was frightening. But Bear paid no attention to the bees. His fur was so thick they couldn't hurt him. He snorted and shook his head and kept eating honey. And finally he filled the two buckets with gobs of golden honeycomb dripping with honey.

"Poor bees," said Woodchuck. "What will
they eat now?"

"Don't worry," said Stork. "They have
plenty left."

Bear walked past his friends. He was
smiling happily. His eyes were wide open, but

75

didn't seem to see anything. The others went behind him. He was taking the honey home. But no—he sat down on the path and put the buckets in front of him, and gobbled it up. Then he picked up the buckets and started back to the bee tree, staggering a little and mumbling, "Buckets."

A long time later, they all arrived at the house, and Bear put two buckets of honey on the table. He had eaten so much honey he could hardly walk, and he felt so good and dizzy he could hardly talk. He sat on the floor in the kitchen and leaned against the wall, and licked the honey off his fur with his long, red tongue.

"Bear," said Stork, "you amaze me."

"Yes," said Bear. He smiled happily and folded his paws on his belly and dropped his chin on his chest and fell asleep.

Everyone tasted the honey, but no one liked it as much as Bear.

"It's not bad," said Dog.

"It's awful," said Bird.

"I wonder why Bear likes the stuff?" said Woodchuck.

"Everyone likes different things," said Stork. "There's no accounting for it."

While Bear slept, they talked about the

harvest feast. It was Stork's turn to cook. He made a batch of young greens and a raspberry pie.

They sat up late that night talking about whom they would invite, and what they would eat, and what games they would play, and what prizes they would give.

And Bear kept sleeping. Or maybe he didn't — they couldn't tell. Every once in a while he would nod and mumble. He seemed to be saying, "Marvelous, marvelous" — but they weren't sure.

Bear still felt good the next day. He took so long to wake up that Woodchuck sat down in the kitchen and watched him. Rabbit came in and said, "What are you doing?" and Woodchuck said, "I'm watching Bear wake up." Rabbit sat down beside him and watched too.

When everybody else woke up, they woke right up. One minute they were asleep, and the next minute they were wide awake. But Bear was different. There seemed to be something delicious inside his body, something as good as honey, and as pleasant as a summer breeze. It was probably golden like honey, and probably hummed and buzzed like the deep still days of

77

summer. He loved to stretch and yawn and just lie there feeling all those good things inside him.

Dog and Cat came into the kitchen, and Dog said, "What are you doing?"

"We're watching Bear wake up," said Rabbit.

Soon all the others came in. Dog went to the pantry and got a bucket of raspberries and passed them around.

Bear's back was propped against the wall. His chin was on his chest, and his paws were folded on his belly.

The bucket of raspberries went from hand to hand.

Bear opened his eyes. He didn't seem to see anything but the sunlight. He breathed deeply and smiled and said, "Um," and closed his eyes.

"Sound asleep," said Rabbit.

"Yep," said Mouse.

Bear opened his mouth without opening his eyes, and said, "Ahhhhhh," and stretched both arms, and stretched them farther and farther, and filled his deep chest with air, and blew it out slowly, saying, "Um," again, and folded his paws on his belly, and dropped his chin on his chest. Maybe he had started a new dream.

"Amazing," said Stork, who always slept standing up.

Bear grunted, and slid down to the floor, and curled into a ball, and said, "Ummm," long and slow. He lay like that for a while. Then he uncurled, and rolled on his back, and stretched out his arms and legs as far as they would go, and opened his mouth and said, "Oh, yes," and then rolled into a ball on the other side, and clacked his tongue in his mouth, and said, "Um," and kept breathing quietly, as if it tasted very good.

"What a pro!" said Cat.

"You have to eat a lot to be able to do that," said Mouse.

"I couldn't stand it," said Squirrel. "Shall I hit him with a nut?"

"No," said Woodchuck.

The bucket of raspberries went from hand to hand, and they sat there quietly and watched Bear sleep. Soon they heard a faint sweet song, a kind of humming that seemed to be coming from far away, and they were amazed to discover that it was coming from Bear.

"Good heavens!" said Stork quietly. "He's singing."

"What song is that?" whispered Woodchuck.

"I don't know the name of it," said Stork.

"I never saw anybody," said Cat, "who could do so many things in his sleep."

They were all talking in whispers.

"I knew a squirrel once," whispered Squirrel, "who climbed trees in his sleep."

"What's the point of that?" whispered Mouse.

"Beats me," whispered Squirrel.

Bear's song got a little louder, and then it stopped. He moved his shoulders without uncurling, arched his strong back, and said, "Yes, yes. Oh, my," and then yawned and uncurled, and rolled on his back, and lay there perfectly flat, saying, "Ahhhhh." He wiggled his toes, and wiggled his feet, and then turned his feet in little circles so that his anklebones crackled. He stretched both legs and said, "Ah," and stretched both arms, and said, "Ah," again. Then he sat straight up and opened his eyes and looked at them.

Bear said nothing. They said nothing.

Bear yawned an enormous yawn, and

looked at them some more. He rubbed his eyes and blinked several times. And then he seemed to notice something that surprised him. "You're up," he said.

What a lot of laughter there was then! Woodchuck clapped his hands and shouted, "Yes, Bear, we're up!"

"Great show," said Cat.

"What's for breakfast?" said Bear.

"Whatever you fix," laughed Stork.

Dog handed him the bucket, and Bear looked into it, but there weren't any raspberries left. They all went out of the house, talking and laughing.

Bear stood up and stretched his great arms, and moved his shoulders around and around. Then, yawning smaller and smaller yawns, he lumbered out into the sunlight.

He stood in front of the house and looked around him. First he squinted and looked at the sun. Then he looked at the tall yellow flowers growing by the window. Then he looked at the garden, which was crowded now with big green leaves and all kinds of things to eat. Then he looked at the trees, which seemed as ripe as the garden, for they were plump and green and crowded with leaves. Then he looked at the brilliant, pale blue sky. He sniffed the air in all directions. Then he scratched his head and sniffed in just one direction. "Hmmm," he said.

"Woodchuck!" he called. "I'll show you something. Help me get buckets."

"Oh, no," said Woodchuck. "Not more honey!"

"Nope," said Bear. "Blueberries."

Woodchuck said, "Oh, boy!" and ran into the house with Bear. They both got buckets and went off into the woods.

In the cool shade of the forest, Woodchuck looked everywhere. He looked under bushes, and behind ferns, and beside rocks. "I don't see any," he said. "Where are they?"

Bear was standing very tall and sniffing the air.

"Blueberries like the sun," he said. "We'll find them on top of a hill, or on a hillside where there aren't any trees."

He left the path and went uphill, picking his way between trees. They walked in a little gully where a stream had flowed in the spring, but now there were ferns and bushes and tiny trees. They climbed a stone wall and walked through more woods, and climbed another wall. There were still some trees, but you could see blue sky between their branches. And then there was a lot of sky, and they were out of the woods, and a broad field sloped upward and leveled at the top. Bear was sniffing deeply and saying, "Aha!" and "Ah." He began to go so fast that Woodchuck could hardly keep up.

The blueberries grew on low, tough little bushes with small green leaves splotched red and brown. They seemed to spread everywhere in the field. Bear ran into their midst and sat down, and by the time Woodchuck caught up with him he was eating berries.

The berries grew in small clusters close to the branches. They were the size of a pea, and were a dusty bright blue, and looked cool. They crunched when you ate them, and the smell was like nothing else in the world. The silvery pale dust that covered them was like the dust on a butterfly's wing, but even finer, so fine it wasn't like dust at all; and if you rubbed it off, the berry was a blue so dark it was almost black.

Woodchuck sat down beside Bear, with his legs apart and the two buckets in front of him. But it was a long time before the *plink* of a berry sounded in the buckets. They ate until they were full, and of course Woodchuck was full first, because Bear's belly was very large and needed hundreds and hundreds of berries to fill it up.

While they ate and filled the buckets, Bear told Woodchuck of all the good things you could make with blueberries, like blueberry muffins, and blueberry pancakes, and blueberry jam, and blueberry pie. And he thought it would be a good idea to put lots of blueberries down in the cellar, and save them for the harvest feast.

"And of course," he said, "we will fill that big crock in the kitchen."

Harvest

First came the harvest, and then came the harvest feast.

It was the end of summer. The days were calm and quiet, for many of the insects were gone, the baby birds had grown, there was no longer the clamor in the trees of nest build-ing and food gathering, and the great green explosion of growing things had come to an end. It was the time of ripeness and harvest.

And how much there was to be picked! There were corn and squash and pumpkins, and green peppers, and broccoli and cabbage and carrots and beets and Swiss chard and lettuce and Brussels sprouts, and two kinds of onions, and three kinds of beans, and four kinds of tomatoes, and five kinds of peas, and six kinds of herbs. Some would be eaten right away, some would keep a short time, and some would last right through the winter.

What a busy time it was! Even busier than the time of planting. And when Woodchuck picked up a head of cabbage, a cabbage so big he had to hold it in both arms, he could not help remembering how tiny the seed had been, and he shook his head in amazement.

Stork remembered everything the farmers had told him. "The cabbages go in the cellar," he said. "The squash and pumpkins go in the attic. We have to dry the onions in the sun a few days. Same for the corn, if we want it to keep. Same for the beans and peas. We'll hang the herbs from the kitchen ceiling."

He showed them how to cook the tomatoes and put them in jars, and the broccoli and the green peppers and Swiss chard. Some of the peas they dried, and some they cooked and put in jars, and some they ate right away.

And some of everything they put aside for the harvest feast.

Bird flew back and forth through the woods

inviting everyone to the feast.

They had all worked hard and were tired, but now they had to sweep and dust and straighten things up.

Squirrel wasn't helping. Squirrel *never*

helped. In fact, they hadn't seen Squirrel for several days.

"I wonder where he is," muttered Stork.

Stork said, "Ouch!" and a nut bounced off his head. Squirrel looked down from his hole in the ceiling and laughed. Then he jumped to the stove, and then to a chair, and then to the table.

"Squirrel," said Stork, "you haven't helped a bit."

Squirrel put his hands on his hips. "Nope," he said.

"We've worked in the garden all summer long," said Rabbit. "What have you done in all that time?"

Squirrel thought for a minute.

"Two thousand forward somersaults," he said.

"Oh," said Woodchuck.

"And two thousand backward somersaults," said Squirrel. "And three thousand flip-flops."

"Ah," said Stork, "but what do you have to show for it?"

Squirrel shrugged.

"What's more to the point," growled Cat, "what do *we* have to show for it?"

"Wonderment!" shouted Squirrel.

He twirled around on the table. He turned a forward somersault, and a backward somersault, and a flip-flop, and jumped onto Cat's head, and bounced from there up to his hole in the ceiling. "Think of me as an acrobat!" he called, and he laughed and popped out of sight.

"Yowr!" roared Cat. "I think of you as a ding-danged comedian! Oh," he said, "wait till I get my dukes on that comedian!"

"Lay off that comedian," Dog growled, "or I'll get my dukes on you."

"What? What? What?" cried Cat. "Get your dukes on *me*? I'm so fast you can't even hit the place where I was! You're lucky to get your dukes on yourself! Get your dukes on me? Put up your dukes!"

Cat hissed and Dog growled, and they bared their teeth.

"Peace! Peace!" said Bear.

"Stop!" said Stork. "No fighting."

"Come on, Stork!" shouted Bird. "No trials, no lawyers, no judges! Let 'em fight it out!"

"Yeah," shouted Mouse. "Squirrel's no comedian!"

"Listen to me, Cat," said Bear. "You too, Dog. Tomorrow, at the harvest feast, you can fight it out. But no biting. Only boxing. And we'll give a prize to the winner."

"I'll be referee," said Stork.

"You can save the trouble," said Cat, "and gimme the prize right now."

"Rowr!" said Dog.

"What about it?" said Bear. "Only boxing."

"If I bit that scrawny piece of fur," growled Dog, "there'd be two tiny cats instead of one noisy small one."

But before Cat could say anything a voice come from the attic.

"Knock, knock," said the voice.

"Pay no attention to him," said Cat.

"Knock, knock," said the voice.

"Who's there?" said Mouse.

"Cat," said the voice.

"I said ignore him," said Cat.

Mouse ducked his head and moved away, but Dog glowered and shouted, "Cat who?"

"Gesundheit!" said the voice, and they could hear Squirrel laughing and rolling on the floor.

"Ha, ha," laughed Dog.

"Ohhhhhh," growled Cat.

"Tomorrow," said Bear. "Save it for tomorrow."

And that was how there came to be a championship prize fight at the harvest feast.

Before they fell asleep that night, Bear said, "Anyway, Squirrel's been working hard all week. I saw him. He's been looking through the woods to see where the nuts are. And he's been fixing a place in the attic to store them. When the time is right, he's a very hard worker."

"Someday," muttered Cat, "I'll get my dukes on that hard worker."

The Harvest Feast

When the first rays of the sun came into the house, they all got up, even Bear, and ate breakfast quickly, and bustled about.

There were buckets and buckets of blueberries. They put them in bowls. The blueberries would be dessert.

And they shelled a lot of peas, and washed a lot of onions, and put a lot of beans in bowls. They washed some carrots and green peppers, and some cabbage and cauliflower and broccoli. But they didn't touch the corn. They left it in the garden. They left some other things there too, so the guests could pick them and eat them on the spot.

Just after lunch the guests began to arrive. They came from everywhere. Birds came flying over the trees, and there were all kinds of them —crows and ducks and blackbirds and robins and sparrows and blue jays and tiny wrens and swallows and finches. Out of the woods came raccoons and deer and skunks and an old porcupine. Up from the ponds and streams came beavers and otters and muskrats. And there was a great milling around and much saying of, "Hello. How are you?" "How do you do?" "Glad to see you." And everyone was excited and wanted to know what games they would play and what races they would run and what prizes they would get. A raccoon asked if there would be any surprises, and Bear said yes, there would be a surprise.

Stork got up on the maple stump and waved his wings for attention.

"Ladies and gentlemen," he said, "friends and neighbors, welcome to the harvest feast."

Everyone cheered, and Woodchuck said, "Good old Stork."

Dog was standing there, growling low in his throat. He curled one paw into a fist and kept smacking it into the other paw.

"The first event," said Stork, "by special request . . ."

"You bet it's special," growled Cat. He was hopping up and down and shooting out his paws in all directions.

". . . will be a championship prize fight between Cat and Dog."

Everyone cheered.

"Which one is the champion?" someone yelled.

And another one called, "Which one is the challenger?"

"They are both champions, and they are both challengers," said Stork, "and they are going to fight it out right now. I will be referee."

There was a great hubbub, and you could hear excited voices saying, "Who's going to win?" "I think Cat will win, he's faster." "No, Dog will win, he's bigger and stronger." "The bigger they come, the harder they fall." "I bet on Cat." "I bet on Dog."

Stork showed them where the prize ring was, and they all ran over and took places around it.

The ring was a square of little stones. Cat and Dog were supposed to fight there and not go outside the ring. In one corner was a chair for Dog to rest in, and in the opposite corner a chair for Cat. Stork stepped into the middle of

the ring and explained that there would be fif-
teen rounds and each round would last three
minutes. During the round Cat and Dog would
fight, and then they would rest on their chairs
for one minute, and then they would fight again.
Stork was holding a bell and he said he would
ring it at the beginning and end of each round.

95

Now Cat and Dog stepped into the ring and sat in their chairs, and Stork made the announcements.

"Laaaa-deeeeeez and gentlemen," he shouted. "In this corner, wearing the striped fur, weighing somewhat less than Dog, the famous pugilist . . . and widely recognized champion/challenger . . . CAT!"

Cat stood up and shook his paws over his head, and danced around and shot out his paws very rapidly in all directions. A great cheer went up. "Hurrah for Cat!" "Cat will win!"

"In this corner," shouted Stork, pointing his wing at Dog, "wearing the light brown fur, weighing somewhat more than Cat, the famous slugger and widely recognized champion/challenger . . . DOG!"

Another cheer went up, and Dog jumped to his feet and made five or six terrific punches whistle through the air. Voices shouted, "Look at those punches!" "What a slugger!" "Hurrah for Dog!" "Dog will win!"

Now Stork called Cat and Dog to the center of the ring and gave them their instructions.

"When I ring the bell," he said, "come out fighting. No biting. When I say break, you better break. When I ring the bell, stop fighting and go to your corners, same corner every time, we don't want Dog in Cat's corner, or Cat in Dog's corner. No punching in the clinches. These are the rules. Where would we be without rules? Chaos would descend upon us. This way we have three-minute rounds. When I ring the bell, commence."

Dog growled, "I'll commence, all right. I'll knock his block off!"

And Cat said, "Ring the ding-danged bell!"

Stork rang the bell and jumped out of the way, and Cat and Dog flew at each other and a great shout went up, and all you could see for a minute was punches flying in all directions, and then Cat danced back lightly and Dog came after him and threw a terrific punch, but Cat ducked under it and hit Dog in the belly, and Dog threw another terrific punch, but Cat jumped back and then jumped forward and hit Dog sixteen times on the side of the head and jumped around in back of Dog, and Dog whirled around and threw a terrific punch very low and Cat jumped over it, and Dog threw a terrific punch very high, and Cat ducked under it, and then Cat hit Dog ten times in the nose with his left hand, and five times on the ear with his right hand, and five times on the other ear with his left hand, and Dog roared and rushed at him, and Cat ducked to one side and hit him twelve times in the belly with his left hand, and ducked to the other side and hit him twelve times in the belly with his right hand, and Dog roared again and rushed straight at him throwing terrific punches first with his right hand and then with his left hand, and Cat hit him ten times in the nose between each punch and ducked them all, and Stork rang the bell and shouted, "Go to your corners!" but they kept right on fighting.

"I'll knock his block off!" roared Dog.

"You can't even see his block!" shouted Cat, and he hit Dog twenty-five times in the nose, and Dog threw a terrific punch, and Cat ducked, and Dog threw another terrific punch, and Cat ducked, and then Cat just stood there and watched Dog throw terrific punches, and then he jumped in and hit Dog thirty-five times on each ear, and Dog roared, "I can't STAND boxing!" and he bared his huge teeth, and opened his jaws wide, and roared a mighty roar, and rushed straight at Cat, and Cat said, "Uh-oh!" and whirled around and dashed out of the ring, and Dog dashed right after him, and chased him right across the garden and across a little field, and Cat scampered up a tree and stood there on a limb looking down, and Dog had both front paws on the trunk of the tree and was barking and barking.

What a lot of talking there was! Everyone went over. Some talked to Dog, and others talked to Cat, and others tried to figure out who had won the fight.

"Cat won the fight," said one, "that's obvious."

"Impossible," said another. "Cat left the ring, so he loses the fight."

"Oh, no," said another, "you aren't allowed to bite in the ring, and Dog was getting ready to bite."

"They both lost," said someone.

"They both won," said someone else.

Dog was standing there huffing and puffing. "What's the prize?" he said. "Gimme the prize."

Bear and Stork put their heads together and talked for a while. Then Stork made an announcement. "Laaaaaaaa-deeeeez and gentlemen," he said. "The winner of the fight is Cat."

A cheer went up.

"Laaaaa-deeeez and gentlemen," said Stork. "The winner of the fight is also Dog."

Another cheer went up.

"Therefore," said Stork, "there will be two first prizes."

"What's the prize?" said Cat, still up in the tree.

"Are you willing to share it?" said Bear. "Are you going to come down?"

"Maybe I am and maybe I'm not," said Cat. "What's the prize?"

"The prize is two blueberry pies," said Bear. "I baked them myself last night. But you have to share them, Cat."

"Blueberry pie!" said Cat, who loved blueberry pie, but didn't know how to bake it.

"Oh, boy!" said Dog, who also loved blueberry pie.

"But you have to share them, Dog," said Bear. "Are you willing to shake hands with Cat?"

"I don't know," said Dog.

"You have to admit," said Bear, "Cat is the fastest one around. Nobody can lay a hand on Cat."

"Well," said Dog, "he better be careful."

"Come down, Cat," said Bear. "And be careful."

So Cat came down, and Stork gave one pie to Cat and the other pie to Dog, and Cat and Dog sat on a big rock and began to eat. Everyone else went away. The next event was to be a running race, and they wanted to hear all about it. But a big, grizzled old deer came over to Cat and Dog and looked at them and said, "In my opinion, you both lost."

Cat and Dog jumped up.

"What do you mean we lost!" said Dog.

"Who asked for your opinion!" said Cat.

"You both lost," said the grizzled old deer. "Neither one of you should get a pie."

Dog punched him a terrific punch on the side of the head, and Cat hit him sixteen times in the nose, and the grizzled old deer shook his head and stepped backward.

"Good heavens!" he said. "It's not safe to express an opinion around here."

"You tried to take away my pie," said Cat. "You call that an opinion?"

"Beat it," said Dog.

The grizzled old deer went away shaking his head, and Dog and Cat sat down on the rock and went back to their pies.

Dog looked at Cat, but said nothing. Cat kept on eating. Dog looked at Cat again, but again said nothing. Then he looked at Cat a third time, and said, "Cat, I've got to hand it to you. You're pretty fast."

Cat swallowed a mouthful of pie. "Thanks," he said. "I notice you're getting faster all the time yourself."

"Am I?" said Dog.

Cat finished eating and stood up. "Sure you are," he said. "Now I'll tell you what, old sport

. . . let's go see about the races."

And that's what they did.

The races were being held in a big field not far from the house. The starting line was at one end of the field and the finish line was at the other, and groups were standing at both ends. Since this was a running race, the birds wouldn't be in it. They were flying back and forth excitedly, looking at the contestants.

"Look at Rabbit," said one of the crows. "I bet he wins."

Rabbit was bounding in the grass, showing off his speed.

"What about Cat?" said another. "He's awfully fast."

"I think Dog is a faster runner," said another.

And then they noticed the big young deer that was going to run, and they watched him gallop around the field getting ready. He looked so handsome and fast and strong, and made such spectacular leaps, that everyone agreed he would surely win.

Now all the runners lined up at the starting line. There were Dog and Cat and Bear and

Woodchuck and Rabbit, and several raccoons, and some otters, and one fat old porcupine who was running just for laughs. And of course there was the handsome big deer who was everybody's favorite.

"Who's going to start us?" asked Dog.

Squirrel jumped on a tree stump and shouted, "I'll start you!"

And so the runners all crouched down to get a fast start, and they waited for Squirrel to say, "Get ready, get set, go!"

But Squirrel said, "G-g-g-g-get r-r-r-r-ready! G-g-g-g-get s-s-s-s-s-set! G-g-g-g-g-g- . . ." and some began to run, and some kept waiting, and Squirrel howled with laughter and jumped into the trees and yelled, "G-g-g-g-g-go!"

All the runners were milling around and yelling at Squirrel. Cat screamed, "Get that

comedian outta here!" and Dog yelled, "Stork! Stork! Come and start us!"

So Stork went over with his wings behind his back, looking very dignified. And the runners lined up again and Stork stood at one end and said, "Runners ready?"

And the runners said, "Ready."

And Stork said, "On your marks."

The runners crouched down.

Stork said, "Get set!"

The runners braced themselves to start as fast as they could.

Stork said, "GO!"—and off they went! All except Bear.

"Go, Bear, go!" said Stork. "Don't you want to win?"

"Oh, I'll win," said Bear. "I'll win." But he just sat there and watched the others.

Cat was out in front because he had started so fast, but soon Rabbit passed him, and then Dog and Deer passed him, and then Cat stopped running and just stood there licking his lips, and the raccoons and otters passed him, and Woodchuck passed him. The fat old porcupine was just lumbering along giggling, and even he passed him, and Cat came strolling back to the starting line, patting his belly and licking his lips.

Dog and Rabbit and Deer were out in front running full tilt. And then Dog passed Rabbit and Deer passed Dog, and everyone was cheering and the birds were flying around shouting, "Come on, Deer! Come on, Deer!" And Deer was halfway down the field . . .

And suddenly Bear shouted, "I'll show you who's too big and clumsy!" And he took off like a streak of lightning.

And what astonishment there was then! For everyone really *had* thought Bear was too big and clumsy. But he moved like a bolt of lightning. First he was all coiled up in a massive ball, then all stretched out like a skinny cat, then all coiled up, then all stretched out, and his back was so strong and his legs were so powerful that clods of grass flew in the air behind him.

Cat blinked. Stork pulled in his chin. It was so amazing that even the cheering stopped. Bear went like a whirlwind. He went so fast the lumbering old porcupine was spun around in the breeze and went off in the wrong direction. Bear caught up with Rabbit and passed him, and caught up with Dog and passed him, and caught up with Deer and passed him, and crossed the finish line, and kept right on going, and ran around the whole field with the grass flying up behind him and the bushes shaking in the breeze. The other runners stopped running and just stood there and watched, it was so amazing.

Bear came to the center of the field and sat down and yawned a big yawn that didn't seem real, and began to clean the dirt out of his toenails as if nobody else were there. But everybody was there. They had all gathered round him, and they were looking at him with their mouths open.

Bear stood up and looked at them and yawned again, and put one hand over his mouth to hide the yawn—but his eyes were twinkling, and when he took his hand away they could see that he was smiling.

Woodchuck said, "Wow, Bear!"

Everyone said, "Wow!"

And then they began to cheer and jump up and down. "Hurrah for Bear!" "I wouldn't believe it if I hadn't seen it!" "Incredible! Just *incredible*!" Bear was dancing from foot to foot and wagging his head and acting silly. And then he shouted, "Hey! What's my prize?"

"Your prize is a promise," said Stork.

"A *promise*?" said Bear. "What can I do with a promise?"

"Well," said Stork, "the apples aren't ripe yet, and the prize is four apple pies. So we promise to give them to you."

"Okay," said Bear. "That's a promise I won't forget." And he rubbed his big paws together and licked his lips, and in his mind was a picture of a cool evening late in September, and the kerosene lamp would be burning in the kitchen, and the windows would be dark and would reflect the golden glow of the little lamp and all the faces of his friends, and the kitchen would be warm with the heat of the stove, and the warmth would smell like apple pies, because apple pies would be baking in the oven, and then someone would take the pies out of the oven and say, "Here you are, Bear—first prize," and Bear would offer to share the pies, but someone would say, "No, Bear, you have to eat them all, because they're a prize," and he would sit down at the table and gobble them up—one, two, three, four, then he would say, "Ahhh! Thank you, my friends," and they would say, "Hurrah for Bear!"

Now there was a flying race for birds, and

Bear said yes, he would be the marker. He stood in the center of the field. The birds would start from there and fly down to Moose's pond and back, and the one to reach Bear first would be the winner.

The birds started stretching their wings and flying over the field, and the others watched them and tried to figure out who would win.

The crows were strong fliers, and some thought they would win, but the ducks were strong fliers, too, and Stork was very strong, and a lot of the smaller birds were very fast.

Bird wasn't warming up, and Woodchuck said to him, "You ought to warm up, Bird. You ought to stretch your wings. Those ducks look pretty fast."

But Bird said, "I'm thinking." And he added, "It's a long way to the pond."

Now Bear clapped his hands and shouted, "Racers to the starting line!" and the birds all flew over and lined up on both sides of him.

Bear said, "Fliers ready?"

The birds said, "Ready."

Bear said, "On your marks!"

And the birds scratched with their feet and wiggled their wings.

Bear said, "Get set!"

The birds bent their knees and thrust their heads forward.

Bear shouted, "GO!"

And off they went! And it sounded as if a thousand hands were clapping. The whole crowd of them soared upward, and you could see them very plainly against the huge white clouds and blue sky.

The smaller birds dashed out in front, but the ducks were right behind them, beating their strong wings as fast as they could. Then came the crows. They weren't trying as hard as the ducks, yet they were going very fast. And then came Stork, and Bird was right behind him, so close you would think the wind from Stork's wings would ruffle his feathers.

"Come on, Bird!" yelled Woodchuck. "Come on, Stork!"

"The ducks will win! Hurrah for the ducks!" cried the raccoons.

"Stork hasn't got a chance," someone said.

"Don't be too sure," said Bear. He was watching Stork closely. Stork's big, powerful wings weren't going very fast, yet he was gaining all the time and, as he gained, his wings went just a bit faster. The impressive thing was

that those powerful wing strokes looked easy.
They looked very, very easy. Cat noticed
it, too.

"Terrific stroke," he said. And then Cat
noticed something odd about Bird. Bird was
flying right behind Stork—they were so close
they were almost touching—yet though Stork's
wings were beating powerfully, Bird's were
scarcely moving at all.

"Now what's that smart little cookie up
to?" said Cat.

You couldn't hear the racers' wings any
more. You could still see them, but they were
getting smaller and smaller. They got as small
as dots, and then you couldn't see them at all,
only the green tops of the trees, the white
clouds, and blue sky.

"The suspense is killing me," said Woodchuck.

"How long will it take?" asked Mouse.

"It's hard to tell," said Bear. "They go a lot
faster through the air than we do on the ground.
And they don't have to go uphill and down, or
swim across streams."

Everyone waited, clustered around Bear.
And while they talked they kept looking over
the treetops where the clouds were drifting

apart and the blue sky was shining through. Some of the deer stopped looking and began nibbling the grass. Cat and Dog sat down and talked, and so did a lot of the others. But Woodchuck climbed on Bear's shoulders and shaded his eyes and looked off into the sky. After a long while he shouted, "Here they come! Here they come!" and they all jumped up and stretched their necks.

All you could see was a swarm of dots low in the sky. The dots got bigger and bigger, and soon you could see birds of all sizes, some flying high and some flying low. The swarm got closer, and the birds got bigger. Someone shouted, "The ducks are in front!"

Right behind the ducks came the swallows, and right behind the swallows came Stork. The crows were even with Stork, but were flying high above him. "Dopes!" said Cat.

Now you could see the birds plainly, and you could see how fast they were going. You could even see that they were getting tired, even Stork, though his wings were beating powerfully and smoothly.

The ducks were still in front. Nobody could catch them. They came to the edge of the field and Bear waved his arms so they'd be sure to see him, and everyone began shouting and cheering.

All of a sudden a little figure whizzed out past Stork, beating his wings so fast you'd think he was just starting out and wasn't tired at all. He caught up to the swallows and whizzed right past them, and caught up to the ducks and whizzed right past them, and whizzed out in front and zoomed down and landed on Bear's head.

It was Bird!

Bird was the winner!

Everyone cheered. All the other birds landed and stood there huffing and puffing, and then they all came over and crowded around Bird, and looked at him in amazement because just to look at he didn't seem that fast or that strong, and he was only a year and a half old. He was hardly even puffing. Yet, sure enough, he had won the race! So after the cheering died down, the other birds congratulated Bird. "Great race, Bird!" "Terrific finish, Bird." But you could also hear them talking among themselves. "I'd never have believed it!" "This younger generation is amazing!" "He's not even winded." "How did he do it?" "Beats me."

Bird was jumping up and down shouting, "I won! I won! What's my prize?"

"We don't know yet," said Bear. "We have to figure it out."

Bear went aside and talked with Stork, and Stork called Cat and Dog and asked them to come too, and then they called Rabbit and Mouse and Woodchuck, and they all stood together and talked in whispers, then they came over to where the crowd was gathered.

"Bird," said Bear, "your prize is this: you get to eat six fat worms out of the garden."

"Worms!" shouted Bird.

"Exactly six," said Stork. "And we will do the counting."

Bird whizzed to the garden, and everyone ran after him and gathered round, and Bird raced up and down the rows listening for worms and scratching and looking closely. He found one and gobbled it up, and Stork said, "One." And Bird gobbled another, and Stork said, "Two." Then everyone began to count, and you could hear a hundred voices shouting, "Three . . . four . . . five . . . SIX!"

Bird flew into the air and turned a somersault and yelled, "Whoopee!"

One of the raccoons remembered that Bear had promised a surprise. "Hey, Bear!" he called. "When are we going to see this surprise o' yours?"

"Right now," said Bear. "Follow me, everybody, if you want a surprise!" He walked off into the woods, and everyone followed him.

On the way to the woods, Cat and Dog sidled up to Bird. Cat smiled and said to Bird, "Like to have a word with you, old sport." They walked slowly and let everyone pass them. Then Cat said, "Okay, Bird, out with it! How'd you manage to win that race?"

Bird looked around to be sure nobody would hear. Then he winked and tapped his head with his wing.

"Come on, Bird," said Cat. "We know you're a smart little cookie. Out with it!"

"Well," said Bird, "it's a long way to the pond."

"That much I know," said Cat.

"And I figured," said Bird, "most of the racers would get tired."

"Yeah, yeah, right," said Cat. "That's not what I call figuring. Go ahead."

"And I figured," said Bird, "that Stork was the strongest flier and would finish near the front."

116

"I figured that too," said Cat. "So what?"

"So here's something you landlubbers don't know," shouted Bird. "A big strong flier like Stork makes a windstream, and if you get right in that windstream you can float along without even moving your wings!"

"Now *that's* what I call FIGURING!" said Cat, and he laughed and patted Bird on the head.

Bird whizzed off to see what Bear's surprise would be, and Cat and Dog strolled along after him.

"Well, well," said Cat.

"Smart little cookie," said Dog.

Shouts and laughter were coming from the woods.

Everybody was gathered in the shade of the trees at the top of a steep little hill. There was a stream at the bottom, with a deep place that was good for swimming. Bear was trudging up the hill with a bucket of water in each hand.

Someone shouted, "You go first, Bear! Show us how it works!"

The otters shouted, "We know how it works! He got the idea from us!"

"No, I didn't," said Bear. "I figured it out myself."

Bear had made a mud slide. It must have taken him quite a while to do it. He had pulled up all the grass and ferns and roots, and had made a long steep trough going right down to the water. He had taken out the stones, and had packed the dirt hard, and had smoothed it. All you had to do was slosh water on it, and it turned into slippery mud.

Bear sloshed both buckets of water onto the slide, and jumped into the air and yelled, "Wahoo!" and landed on his back and went zipping downhill with all four feet in the air. He made an enormous splash in the stream. He clambered out, and someone else yelled, "Wahoo!" and went zipping down. There was laughter everywhere. And of course the otters did know all about mud slides. They slid down hundreds of ways, and invented such funny tricks that everyone laughed again and again.

But the most spectacular trick was Bear's. It was called The Cannonball. He would go back a little way, and come running full speed right up to the slide, and leap nose first into the air, but before he landed, he curled into a ball, and the ball went rolling downhill and splashed into the stream with a mighty PLOSH!

The birds, of course, just stood and watched. They made faces at each other and yawned and looked at the clouds. Cat leaned against a tree and said that water sports were not his dish of tea. But everyone else slid and somersaulted and splashed and frolicked.

And they got hungrier and hungrier, and all of a sudden, though not a single word had been spoken, everyone understood that it was time to eat. They splashed up and down in the water and washed off all the mud, and shook themselves, and felt tingly and relaxed and happy, and went off together to begin the harvest feast.

Stork flew ahead of them so that he could

greet them again near the garden. "Go right to the garden, my friends," he said. "The *hors d'oeuvres* are in the garden. Just help yourselves. *Hors d'oeuvres* are in the garden. I recommend the peas. I recommend the cucumbers, too. I recommend the lettuce, and also the chard. Also the broccoli and cauliflower. Hmm. Yes. As a matter of fact, just help yourselves, my friends."

Everyone ran into the garden. And such a buzz there was of chewing and chatter, and chatter and chewing! They wandered along the rows and sampled this and sampled that, and passed things to each other, and said, "Excellent!" and "Awfully good!" and "Thank you," and "Have some more." The gardeners were very pleased to hear so many compliments, and they complimented each other, and began to say, "Awfully good!" and "Excellent!" and "Thank you, have some more."

While they were eating, they realized that Moose hadn't come to the party.

Bird had taken around the invitations. Dog turned to him and said, "Bird, are you sure you invited him?"

"Sure I'm sure," said Bird. "I invited him twice, and I even said, 'You won't forget, will you?' and he said, 'Thank you, little Bird, I'll be happy to come.' "

"But he hasn't come," said Mouse.

"The party's not over," said Cat.

While the others were eating, Bear and Stork made an enormous fire in the little field beside the house. The sun was still bright, but was low in the sky. The great flames of the fire wavered and made heat-shimmers in the air.

"Why," said Rabbit, "you can't stand near a fire that big. How are we going to cook on it?"

"We're not," said Dog. "We'll let it die down until only ashes and glowing coals are left, and then we'll put the corn in the coals with the husks still on."

"Right," said Cat. And he explained to Rabbit, "You've never eaten corn till you've eaten it roasted in the husk."

"And you pick it at the very last minute," said Dog. "Otherwise you've never eaten corn."

"I see," said Rabbit. And he explained it to someone else, and soon everyone knew that the special feature of the harvest feast would be corn picked at the very last minute and roasted in the husk, and they rubbed their hands and licked their lips, and watched the fire, which was slowly dying down.

Bear and Stork came running to the garden. "Pick corn!" Bear shouted. "Pick corn!"

They all ran among the tall stalks of corn and picked as many ears as they wanted, and ran with them to the fire. Bear took a stick and pulled and pushed at the glowing coals until there was a clear space in the middle. He laid the corn there and covered it with grass, then pushed the ashes and coals on top of it, and then sat down with the others. Soon gray-white

clouds of smoke billowed from the fire, and a few minutes later the smoke began to smell delicious.

"Ahhh!" said Cat. "Catch that aroma!"

Just then they heard steady, heavy footsteps on the forest path, and then it seemed as if a broad-branched tree were stepping out of the woods all by itself.

"Moose!"

"Hello, Moose!"

"It's Moose!"

Moose stood there by the trees and bowed his head to them, and came forward slowly as they ran to meet him.

"Moose!" cried Bear. "You're just in time for roasted corn. And after the corn I have a surprise."

"Another surprise?" said Woodchuck.

"Come see the garden, Moose," cried Stork. "There are still some *hors d'oeuvres*, I mean peas and beans and everything you can name."

"Except water lilies, Moose," said Cat.

"Come see the house, Moose," cried Woodchuck. "See how we've fixed it up."

"But it's time to eat," said Bear. "Let Moose eat first, and then we can show him the house."

"Yes," said Moose. "Thank you."

Moose greeted everyone, and then he went

with the gardeners to look at the garden.

"How do you like it, Moose?" said Woodchuck.

"Excellent," said Moose. "You have done very well."

Stork brought him some beans and said, "Try these!" Dog brought him some peas and lettuce and said, "Try these!" Cat brought him some broccoli and cabbage and said, "Try these!"

Moose tried them all, nodding while he munched, and said, "Excellent. First rate."

They went back to the fire where the other guests were gathered. Bear took the long stick and pushed the coals away and pulled the corn out of the fire. He picked up an ear and said, "Moose, the first one is for you."

Moose nodded and said, "Thank you." He held up the ear of corn so that everyone could see it, and stripped off the husks with his teeth. Then he munched it, and nodded, and said, "Excellent." Bear and Stork and Dog passed out corn to everybody, and on all sides you could hear, "Delicious!" "Wow!" "Terrific corn!" and "You haven't eaten corn till you've eaten it roasted in the husk!" All you could hear then was munching and sighing. The raccoons, especially, were very pleased.

They passed around the food they had prepared that morning—onions, and green peppers, and tomatoes, and carrots. And Bear stood up and said, "A little surprise." He took the long stick and dug it in the ground where the fire had been, and out popped baked potatoes and baked squash. He had buried them before he built the fire, and now they were tender and steaming and filled the air with marvelous smells.

Soon you could hear voices saying, "What a feast!" "I'm so full I couldn't eat another bite!" "I'm so full I can hardly move." "Have some more." "Thank you."

The guests lay on the grass in little groups and talked of the races that afternoon, and the boxing match, and the marvelous mud slide.

Stork said, "Ladies and gentlemen, we will serve dessert presently, so don't go to sleep."

"Dessert?" someone said. "I couldn't eat another bite. What is it?"

"I will give you a hint," said Stork. "It's delicious."

Stork and Bear and Dog and Cat and Woodchuck all went to the house to get the dessert, and Moose went with them to see the house. Of course he wouldn't go inside; he was much too big. But he would look in the windows.

He was just reaching the window when Squirrel jumped up on the sill.

"Squirrel!" said Bear. "Why didn't you come to the feast?"

"I've been eating nuts," said Squirrel, "but I'll join you for dessert." And he said, "How do you do," to Moose.

"Do you live here?" said Moose.

"This is my house," said Squirrel. "These poor gardeners had no place to live, so I took them in. They've been working hard all summer, the dopes."

"Oh?" said Moose. "And how do you spend *your* days?"

Squirrel laughed and yelled, "Alley oop!" He turned a somersault, and then a flip-flop, and then another somersault, and then a double flip-flop.

And Moose smiled the biggest smile anyone had ever seen.

"Jump into my antlers, little Squirrel," he said, and Squirrel did, and sat there proudly. Moose looked in all the windows of the house, and talked with Squirrel. Then Bear and Stork and Dog and Cat and Woodchuck came out of the house, carrying heavy baskets and big buckets, and they all went together to join the guests.

The buckets and baskets were full of blueberries. There were blueberry muffins, too, and blueberry pies. And there were raspberry pies, and blackberry pies, and rhubarb pies, and elderberry pies.

Bear was smiling.

Woodchuck said, "You get so stuffed you can't eat another mouthful, but then along comes a blueberry pie and you eat the whole thing."

The guests were lying and sitting on the grass, talking busily. Some told of events in the woods, others told of the fields, and still others of the ponds and streams. The raccoons said they expected a hard winter and were glad of the chance to eat heavily because that would help them sleep it out. And the birds said yes, it would be a hard winter. They were planning to fly south a bit earlier this year.

All the pies and muffins and blueberries were passed around, and again there were compliments on all sides, and the gardeners were saying, "Thank you, thank you." Stork got dizzy hearing so many compliments and instead of just saying "Thank you" he began to say, "Yes, indeed. Thank you. Yes, indeed," and Woodchuck said, "Uh-oh, he's going to run for president again," but Bear said, "No, I don't think so." He explained to Woodchuck that you simply can't make speeches after a heavy dinner, because nobody would listen. They would just fall asleep.

The sun was going down. It was almost touching the hills. It was very large, and very red, and very round.

Bear and Dog made another fire, one to gather round and look at and feel warm by, and everyone gathered round it. Squirrel was still sitting in Moose's antlers. They were talking. Now all the gardeners stood together by the fire, and sang a song they had been practicing. The words were by a poet named Blake. It was about a nurse and all the children she cared for.

When the voices of children
are heard on the green
And laughing is heard on the hill,
My heart is at rest within my breast
And everything else is still.

"Then come home, my children, the sun
is gone down
And the dews of night arise;
Come, come, leave off play,
and let us away
Till the morning appears in the skies."

And then the children answered the nurse,

and the singers made their voices sound like the voices of children.

> *"No, no, let us play,*
> *   for it is yet day*
> *And we cannot go to sleep;*
> *Besides, in the sky the little birds fly*
> *And the hills are all covered with sheep."*

And the nurse sang again to the children,

> *"Well, well, go and play till the light*
> *   fades away*
> *And then go home to bed."*
> *The little ones leaped and shouted*
> *   and laughed*
> *And all the hills echoed.*

Everyone was quiet for a while, and then all the birds, without even talking it over, began to sing together. They sang in chorus, and then with alternating choruses and solos, and then with many solos woven together and spaced by choruses, and it was very grand and beautiful, and just as it was dying out it was lifted by a great new wave of music that took everyone by surprise, for hundreds of frogs and crickets had gathered in the shadows beyond the fire and they thrummed and chirped, and inspired the birds to keep singing.

That song, too, was too beautiful to say anything about, and after a time of silence one of the otters shouted, "Play some circus music!" The musicians struck up merrily, and the music was fast and bouncy and gay. It sounded like laughter and made you want to tap your feet and dance. Five otters came wiggling and bounding into the clear space by the fire, and they barked with laughter and clapped their hands, and turned somersaults and juggled stones and did headstands, and chased each other, and there were shouts of "Bravo! Bravo!" and delighted laughter.

When the otters were finished, someone said, "Bear, tell us a story." And someone else said, "Yes, Bear, do."

Bear was famous for his stories. He never made them up. They all came to him in dreams during the long sleep of winter, and when he told these stories he always began by saying, "I dreamed once..."

He stepped into the clear space by the fire, and looked around at everyone, and cocked his head and thought for a minute, and then said,

"I dreamed once there was an old crow who was a magician. He got a fish bone stuck in his throat and was going to die, but a little caterpillar crawled down his throat and got it out for him. So the old crow said, 'Make any wish you want, just one wish, and I will grant it to you.'

"The caterpillar thought for a long time. She knew that soon she would spin her cocoon and go to sleep inside it, and then the cocoon would open and she would come out again and be a butterfly, and then would lay her eggs, and after that would die. And she thought, 'If I could spin a magic cocoon, and be anything I want when I come out, any creature at all, a bird, or a fish, or a deer, and then spin my magic cocoon whenever I wanted, I would never have to die, never at all.'

"And so the caterpillar told the old magician exactly what she wanted. The crow looked at her a long time and said nothing. Then finally the crow said, 'Very well,' and showed her how to spin a magic cocoon. And she spun one immediately, and when she came out she was a bird, and she flew into the sky, and marveled at the clouds, and learned to ride the wind, and lived like that for many years, and grew old and weak, and a mighty windstorm hurled her against a tree and broke her wings. She thought that she would die. She said, 'Magic cocoon, change me to a deer!'

"And the cocoon spun itself around her, and when she came out she was a frisky young deer, and ran prancing through the woods, and learned how to search for grass and wild vegetables and the tender bark of evergreens in the wintertime, and then it was time to die, and she said, 'Magic cocoon, change me to a fish,' and the cocoon spun itself around her and she became a fish, and after that an elephant, and then a monkey, and then a mouse, and then a tiger, and then a bear, and then a horse. She became all creatures in the world, even bugs, and the world rolled on and on and was so old it could not be counted, and there was nothing left to be, she had been every creature that exists, and the last one was a crocodile, and she grew old and weak and it was time to die. She was not sure that she wanted to do it all again. She tried to figure it out. She decided to find the old magician and ask his advice, but he had died long, long ago, so long ago it could not be counted, and she wondered what to do. While she lay there on the bank of the river she saw a little caterpillar and was astonished, for she had seen him before, she knew him, she had known him in the woods when she herself had been a caterpillar. She said, 'I know you! I saw you long, long ago!' 'No,' said the caterpillar, 'you couldn't have. I have only just been born.' 'I'm positive,' she said, 'there's no mistake!' But the caterpillar shook his head and said, 'I have only just been born.'

"And then she knew what she would do. She said, 'Magic cocoon, change me to a caterpillar.' And the cocoon spun itself around her, and she came out a caterpillar, and ate the leaves of plants and slept at night curled in the ground, and the time came to spin a real cocoon, and she did, and came out a butterfly, and flew in the bright sunlight a short while, and laid her eggs, and soon felt the end of her life spreading quietly through her, and she lay on the ground and beat her wings feebly, and then dropped her head and died."

Bear sat down. Someone coughed. Someone else said, "Thank you, Bear." Another said, "Good." They were speaking quietly.

Woodchuck whispered, "Gee, Bear, is that story true?"

Bear said, "I don't know."

Soon there was more talking and then there

was a lot of talking, and you could hear voices saying "Hmmm. I don't know," and "Maybe so, and then again maybe not."

Squirrel and Moose stood off to one side talking busily. Squirrel was perched on a tree stump. Moose held his head low. Squirrel nodded several times and rubbed his hands. Then Moose talked to the musicians, and presently a sweet music rose out of the grass just the way darkness rises at dusk, flowing upward from the grass to the trees and then climbing the sky.

Moose stepped into the space by the fire. The music grew quiet and died out.

Moose said, "Squirrel and I will do a play."

Squirrel stood near him.

Moose waved his head slowly from side to side.

"My right antler is the sun," he said, "my left the moon. See how they follow each other through the sky."

He waved his head slowly. "Now watch," he said, "and you will see how the clouds sail back and forth, and how the Milky Way glows, and how falling stars plunge down and go dark."

Squirrel leaped to his antlers, and soared back and forth like the flying clouds, and did his best to glow like the Milky Way, for he spread his fingers and made them twinkle while he soared from antler to antler, and made his eyes twinkle, too, and his teeth shine, and turned such remarkable somersaults that everyone called them brilliant, and then he leaped into the air, all a-sparkle, and fell out of sight behind a bush, just like a falling star.

There were shouts of *Bravo! Bravo!* And Squirrel and Moose did it all again, but this time with music, for the frogs and crickets began to play, and the birds to sing, and Squirrel outdid himself, he did soaring flip-flops and quadruple somersaults that almost made you dizzy to watch, and the slow, steady waving of Moose's head began to seem like a deep, slow song, or like a dance so perfectly right there was no reason ever to change it or ever to stop. But they did change it. After Squirrel dropped like a falling star, he came strutting out, and stood in the grass as tall as he could, which wasn't very tall, and said, "My right ear is the sun, my left ear is the moon." He held up his head, but his ears were so small scarcely anyone could see them. And Moose said, "I will soar back and forth like the flying clouds." He tried to get on Squirrel's head, but couldn't find him, and

Squirrel frolicked between his legs, and turned somersaults, and they spun round and round, and Moose cried, "Hold still, sun! Where are you, moon?" And Squirrel shouted, "Here I am, clouds! Where are you, clouds?" and the musicians played a wild, funny music, and there was laughter everywhere, and then the music stopped, and Squirrel and Moose made very low bows, and there was laughter again, and then Dog and Bear and Stork walked among the guests with their baskets, urging them to eat more pie, but scarcely anyone did; they were content to just lie there and look at the fire and watch the moon come up.

The moon was full. It was as round as the sun and was dazzlingly white.

Moose walked away from the fire, and turned and faced everyone.

"I have enjoyed your feast," he said. "Please invite me to your next one."

Many voices called, "Good night, Moose, good night," and all the gardeners ran to him and said good night and thanked him for coming and urged him to visit whenever he liked.

Moose nodded solemnly and walked a few steps away. He turned to them and said, "Good night to you all," and then vanished into the shadows of the woods. They could hear the heavy, even tread of his feet. And then his footsteps stopped, and his voice called out from the darkness, "Good night, sweet Squirrel."

"Good night, sweet Moose," called Squirrel.

Moose's footsteps could be heard again, growing fainter and fainter, and finally there was only the silence of the woods.

Now all the guests began to leave. They thanked their hosts, and drifted into the woods. All the deer went together, and the raccoons, and the otters, and all the birds. Some of the guests had fallen asleep. They woke up when they heard the others going, and jumped up yawning, and said good night, and scampered off. "A perfect feast," they said. "A marvelous feast." Some even called, "Good night! Good night!" from the depths of the woods. And many of the birds, who would soon be flying south, called back, "See you next year."

For a while it seemed empty and lonely in the little field beside the house. Bear put more wood on the fire.

"I suppose," said Stork, "we should clean the buckets and pots and pans." But he just stood there and seemed too sleepy to move.

"I feel too good to do anything at all," said Dog.

And apparently they all felt that way, for no one moved.

Then Squirrel said, "Good night," and Mouse said, "Good night," and Bird said, "Good night," and they went off to the house, wobbling with sleepiness. Rabbit was already sound asleep in the grass.

Bear leaned against a tree and crossed his hands on his belly and said, "Ahhhh."

"Yes," said Stork.

Woodchuck sat beside Bear, and Dog and Cat stretched out in the grass. The fire was bright and warm.

"What a fabulous moon!" said Bear.

"Yes," said Stork. He opened his eyes and looked at it gravely. Dog and Cat looked at it too, and so did Woodchuck.

"Who would think to invent such a thing?" said Bear. "What a simple shape it is! Yet how pleasant!"

"Simple?" said Woodchuck. "I still don't know what makes it hang there. And what do you suppose makes it move? And how do they keep it from wobbling?"

"It's as handsome as an onion," said Bear.

Cat was snoring, and Dog said, "Listen to him snore."

"I'm thinking about what you said," said

Stork. He was standing on one leg and his eyes were closed.

"I found a whole box of green beans by somebody's barn once," said Woodchuck. "Another nice thing is to sleep right through the winter."

"Yes," said Bear.

Dog was snoring too.

"Did you ever see a young, tasty cabbage," said Woodchuck, "that was bigger than a big old cabbage?"

"No," said Bear.

"Too bad," said Woodchuck. And he too fell asleep.

The moon was high in the sky now, and the fire was dying down. Bear looked at his friends.

"They are all asleep," he said.

And then he said, "A night like this is too good to waste on sleep. I'll just stay here and watch it."

But Bear, too, fell asleep. He fell asleep and dreamed he was leaning against a tree watching the night, and a harvest moon was shining down, and Cat and Dog and Stork and Woodchuck were sound asleep all around him.